Market
mercado

Carmen Parks

Illustrated by /Ilustrado por
Edward Martinez

Translated by/Traducido por
F. Isabel Campoy y Alma Flor Ada

Green Light Readers   Colección Luz Verde

sandpiper

Houghton Mifflin Harcourt
Boston   New York

It's still dark, but it's time for me to get up. It's market day in Red Rock.

Todavía está oscuro, pero ya es hora de levantarme. Hoy es día de mercado en Red Rock.

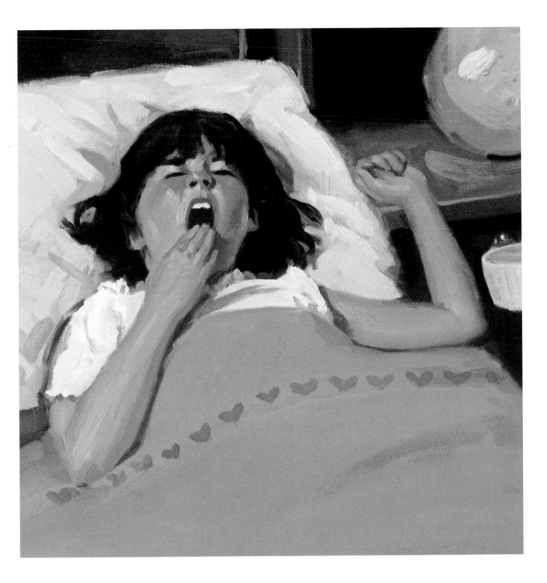

Letter from the Translators

Dear Readers,

We frequently bring our talk "The Magical Encounter Between Books and Children" to readers' communities, and wherever we are, we try to introduce children to books. When a child has found a friend in the pages of a book, that child is already on the path to academic success.

Professionally, we come from the fields of applied linguistics and education, areas in which we have published extensively and on which we have lectured in universities around the world. Personally, we are both daughters of the imagination and friends of discovery. As children's authors we have published hundreds of books, and because we are bilingual, we love to share the treasures hidden in the books of English- and Spanish-speaking authors, which we had an opportunity to do as consultants on the Green Light Readers/Colección Luz Verde series.

It was a pleasure to select these excellent stories with great illustrations for beginning readers and make them available in Spanish in words as engaging as those used in the originals. For the Spanish-speaking child, it will be significant to have access to authentic texts by recognized authors and illustrators in the United States. For the child learning Spanish, it is essential for the language to be not only correct but inspiring.

The early experiences between children and books are key to their future success. Opening the door of wonder, magic, fun, and knowledge through the printed word is the first step for children in loving the world that reading will bring to their lives. With bilingual books, a universal mind can be fostered at very early ages. That is the world our children will need, and we are helping them to get there.

¡Felicidades!

Alma Flor Ada & F. Isabel Campoy

Farmers
Día de

I always go to the market with Mom and Dad. We sell fruits and vegetables from our farm.

Siempre voy al mercado con mamá y papá. Vendemos frutas y verduras de nuestra granja.

We have to get up early because
the market is far away.

Tenemos que levantarnos temprano
porque el mercado está lejos.

As we start out this morning,
the stars are still shining.

Esta mañana, cuando salimos,
todavía brillaban las estrellas.

At last we get to Red Rock. We park the truck in the big lot and then set up our cart.

Por fin llegamos a Red Rock. Estacionamos el camión en la explanada y montamos nuestro puesto.

We have lots of fruits and vegetables
to sell.

Tenemos muchas frutas y verduras
para vender.

"This corn smells fresh," a man says.
"These eggplants look fresh, too."

—Este maíz huele fresco—dice un hombre.
—Estas berenjenas también parecen frescas.

Lots of people stop at our cart.
My best friend, Carmen, stops by.

Mucha gente para en nuestro puesto.
Carmen, mi mejor amiga, viene a verme.

Carmen fills her arms with corn.
She gets some lemons, too.

Carmen se llena los brazos con mazorcas
de maíz. Compra tambíen unos limones.

Dad sells the last of the corn.
Now nothing is left on the cart!

Papá vende todo el maíz que queda.
¡Ya no queda nada en el puesto!

Market day is over. We pick up the trash and go back home.

Se acabó el día de mercado. Recogemos la basura y regresamos a casa.

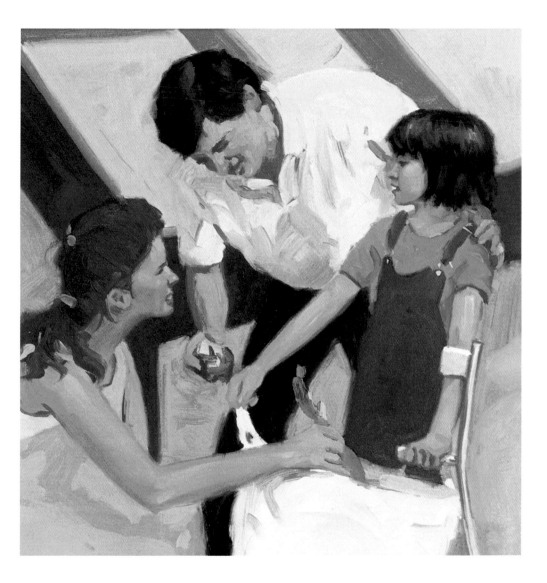

Market days always go by fast.
I think I like market days the best!

Los días de mercado pasan muy deprisa.
¡Creo que los días de mercado son los
mejores!

Your Own Market

Make some food to sell at
your own market!

WHAT YOU'LL NEED

paper

tape

scissors

crayons or markers

1 Draw pictures of different foods. Cut them out.

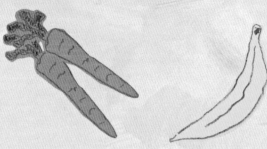

2 Make some price tags. Tape them to the food.

3 Ask a friend to come to your market. Take turns buying and selling the food.

Tu propio mercado

Haz algunos alimentos para vender en tu propio mercado.

LO QUE VAS A NECESITAR

papel

cinta adhesiva

tijeras

lápices de colores o marcadores

1 Haz dibujos de varios alimentos. Recórtalos.

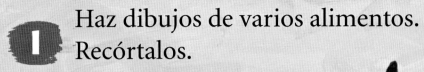

2 Haz etiquetas con los precios. Pégalas a los alimentos.

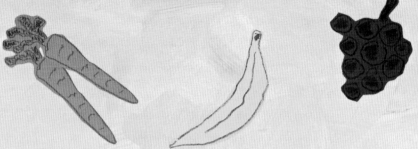

20¢

5¢

10¢

3 Invita a alguien a venir a tu mercado. Cambien los papeles de quien compra y quien vende.

© 2001 Rick Falco/Black Star

Edward Martinez (signature)

Meet the Illustrator

Edward Martinez loves to paint. He began his work on *Farmers Market* by taking pictures of real children. Then he looked at the photos as he painted the children in the story. Look closely—the kids might be based on someone you know!

Conoce al ilustrador

A Edward Martinez le encanta pintar. Empezó su trabajo en *Día de mercado* tomando fotos de niños. Dibujó a los niños del cuento mirando esas fotos. Fíjate bien, es posible que estos personajes estén basados en alguien que tú conozcas.

About the translators

F. Isabel Campoy and Alma Flor Ada have written more than a hundred books each, and each has translated many books also. But they enjoy writing and translating books in collaboration. It's great fun!

Sobre las traductoras

F. Isabel Campoy y Alma Flor Ada han escrito más de cien libros cada una, y cada una también ha traducido muchos libros. Pero les encanta cuando pueden escribir o traducir libros entre las dos. ¡Es muy divertido!

www.hmhco.com

First Green Light Readers/Colección Luz Verde edition 2010

SANDPIPER and the SANDPIPER logo are trademarks of
Houghton Mifflin Harcourt Publishing Company.

Green Light Readers and its logo are trademarks of
Houghton Mifflin Harcourt Publishing Company,
registered in the United States of America and/or other jurisdictions.

Library of Congress Cataloging-in-Publication Data is on file.

ISBN 978-0-547-36899-3
ISBN 978-0-547-36900-6 (pb)

Printed in China
SCP   17 16 15 14 13 12 11
4500527326

Ages: 5–7
Grades: 1–2
Guided Reading Level: G–H
Reading Recovery Level: 14-15

Green Light Readers
For the reader who's ready to GO!

Five Tips to Help Your Child Become a Great Reader

1. Get involved. Reading aloud to and with your child is just as important as encouraging your child to read independently.

2. Be curious. Ask questions about what your child is reading.

3. Make reading fun. Allow your child to pick books on subjects that interest her or him.

4. Words are everywhere—not just in books. Practice reading signs, packages, and cereal boxes with your child.

5. Set a good example. Make sure your child sees YOU reading.

Why Green Light Readers Is the Best Series for Your New Reader

• Created exclusively for beginning readers by some of the biggest and brightest names in children's books

• Reinforces the reading skills your child is learning in school

• Encourages children to read—and finish—books by themselves

• Offers extra enrichment through fun, age-appropriate activities unique to each story

• Incorporates characteristics of the Reading Recovery® program used by educators

• Developed with Harcourt School Publishers and credentialed educational consultants

Colección Luz Verde
¡Para los lectores que están listos para AVANZAR!

Cinco sugerencias para ayudar a que su niño se vuelva un gran lector

1. Participe. Leerle en voz alta a su niño, o leer junto con él, es tan importante como animar al niño a leer por sí mismo.

2. Exprese interés. Hágale preguntas al niño sobre lo que está leyendo.

3. Haga que la lectura sea divertida. Permítale al niño elegir libros sobre temas que le interesen.

4. Hay palabras en todas partes, no sólo en los libros. Anime a su niño a practicar la lectura leyendo carteles, anuncios e información, como en las cajas de cereales.

5. Dé un buen ejemplo. Asegúrese de que su niño vea que USTED lee.

Por qué esta serie es la mejor para los lectores que comienzan

● Ha sido creada exclusivamente para los niños que empiezan a leer, por algunos de los más brillantes e importantes creadores de libros infantiles.

● Refuerza las habilidades de lectura que su niño está aprendiendo en la escuela.

● Anima a los niños a leer libros de principio a fin, por sí solos.

● Ofrece actividades de enriquecimiento, entretenidas y apropiadas para la edad del lector, creadas para cada cuento.

● Incorpora características del programa Reading Recovery® usado por educadores.

● Ha sido desarrollada por la división escolar de Harcourt y por consultores educativos acreditados.